by
Don Conroy

MENTOR
BOOKS

This Edition first published 1999 by

MENTOR BOOKS
43 Furze Road
Sandyford Industrial Estate
Dublin 18
Tel. + 353 1 295 2112/3   Fax. + 353 1 295 2114
e-mail: admin@mentorbooks.ie
website: www.mentorbooks.ie

ISBN: 1-902586-52-2

A catalogue record for this book is available from the
British Library

Cover Illustration: Don Conroy
Editing, Design and Layout by Mentor Books

Printed in Ireland by ColourBooks Ltd.

1 3 5 7 9 10 8 6 4 2

The W-Files

Hatti

Grimly   Abbiewail   Scarea

Dedicated
to
Sophie

The W-Files

'Oh fiddlesticks,' Abbiewail grumbled.

'What's the matter, sister?' Grimly asked.

'I'm getting very bad reception on my crystal ball. There's all kinds of interference on it.'

'Let me see,' Grimly offered. She took out a blue piece of velvet and polished the crystal ball. 'There that's better, it's always good to clean the surface.'

'Thank you, Grimly. I'll try to make contact with Flawless again. Hello. Are you there, Flawless? It's your first cousin once removed, Abbiewail. Over.'

Grimly and Abbiewail could see a lot of thunder and lightning in the ball, then a strange bright object could be seen passing through the clouds.

'How very odd,' said Grimly.

'Odd! You're telling me! It's been like that all morning. There must be interference on the psychic waves.'

Boris the raven flew over and landed on Abbiewail. 'Anything good on the box?'

'Listen, bird brain . . . it's not a television, it's a very special accessory for witches.'

'What does it do?' Boris asked.

'It finds out things for me, or helps me communicate with friends or relatives both near and far.'

'Did you ever hear of a telephone?' Boris asked innocently.

'Yes!' snapped Abbiewail. 'But this is far superior than any telephone, or television for that matter.'

'Can you get all the channels?' asked Boris.

'National Geographic? Sky Sports? Discovery?'

'Well, no,' said Abbiewail. 'But I can get all the psychic channels, The Astral World, for example.'

'Never heard of it,' the raven quipped. 'I suppose it's full of bad news and repeats.'

'Breakfast's ready,' Scarea announced as she entered the room with Meaty the vulture on her shoulder.

'I love that magic word,' said Meaty. 'Breakfast.'

'Me too,' Boris added.

They all gathered round the table.

Hatti flew in the kitchen window on her broom. 'Good morning all,' she said brightly, as she screeched to a halt. Then, parking her broom, she hurried to the breakfast table.

'I wish you wouldn't come in like that,' Abbiewail grumbled. 'You cause such a cold draught.'

'Oops sorry, Auntie,' said Hatti.

'Who got out of the wrong side of the bed this morning?' Fangy the bat remarked.

'Oh don't be too hard on dear Abbiewail. She's been trying for ages to send a Happy 4th of July greeting to our cousins Flawless and Rosalind living in Salem in America. But there's such bad reception on the crystal ball . . .'

'It's been like that all morning,' Abbiewail sighed.

'Why not send them an e-mail?' Hatti suggested.

'E-mail? Is that one of those new-fangled ideas?' Hatti nodded. 'No thanks, Hatti, I'll stick to my crystal ball.'

'You've got to move with the times,' said Scarea as she buttered her toast.

'Move with the times?' said Abbiewail 'I've a broomstick that will move me anywhere into the future or the past, so there.'

'Well said, Abbiewail,' Grimly chuckled.

Hatti watched the raven and the vulture squabble over a piece of toast. 'Birds, please behave, there's plenty of breakfast for everyone and if there isn't,' she winked, 'I'll magic up some more.'

Meanwhile Chompy the tarantula crawled over to the crystal ball and began to stare at it. Then he gave a loud shriek.

'What on earth is the matter?' snapped Scarea. 'Shrieking like that . . .'

The spider quickly scurried down the side of the desk, across the floor then up the leg of the kitchen table. He was panting hard.

'It's at times like these I wish I had wings.'

'What's up?' asked Hatti.

'Well I heard a funny noise coming from the crystal ball so I went over to investigate. Then I saw this horrible creepy-crawly type of creature.'

'See! There is something wrong with that crystal ball,' declared Abbiewail triumphantly.

They all hurried over and peered into the magic ball.

'Look!' said Grimly in excited tones. 'I can see Flawless.'

Their cousin seemed to be in a haze of green light and was saying 'ROSWELL'.

'Hello Flawless. Happy 4th of July. This is Grimly. Can you hear me, dear?'

'ROSWELL' – the word could be heard faintly, coming from the crystal ball.

'Oh isn't that just like Flawless, thinking of others first. Rosalind her sister is keeping well.' Grimly beamed.

'That's not what cousin Flawless said,' Scarea remarked.

'Whatever do you mean?' said Grimly. 'I distinctly heard "Ros is well".'

'No, sister Grimly, she clearly said "ROSWELL",' Scarea insisted.

'What's the difference?' snapped Abbiewail. 'Why do you have to be so precise all the time?'

'Because Flawless never refers to her sister as Ros . . . always Rosalind.'

'Excuse me, Aunties,' Hatti piped up. 'But Roswell is the name of a place in America.'

'That young child has brains to burn,' Meaty quipped.

The raven nodded in agreement.

'Quiet!' said Abbiewail. 'Another message is coming through on the crystal ball. Oh look,' she chuckled, 'it's dear Rosalind. See?' She pointed at the circular glass.

Rosalind too was wrapped in a green haze. 'Kidnapped. Kidnapped . . .' Their cousin's voice trailed off.

'What did she say?' asked Abbiewail.

'I think she said she's having a catnap,' Grimly offered.

'Oh,' said Abbiewail. 'I must have disturbed her sleep. What time is it in America?'

'You two are impossible! She said "kidnapped",' sighed Scarea.

Then it began to dawn on them what the message meant. They called out in unison 'KIDNAPPED!!!'

'Oh my,' said Grimly. 'Who would want to kidnap our cousins, Flawless and Rosalind?'

'There'll be a ransom, I suppose . . .' Scarea added.

'What can we give?' said Abbiewail nervously. 'I hope they don't want my new witch's hat or my broomstick.'

'Don't be ridiculous,' Scarea scolded.

'Look,' said Hatti. 'There's something very strange appearing in the crystal ball.'

'Hey, that's what I saw earlier,' said Chompy.

They all gave out a loud shriek, for inside the crystal ball the image of an alien could be seen clearly. Then it vanished and all that remained were bright, pulsating lights. After a while the crystal ball was clear again.

'Well whatever it was it's gone now,' said Grimly.

'I wasn't scared,' said Abbiewail hiding behind Grimly.

'Oh dear, what are we to do?' sighed Grimly.

The three sisters paced up and down the room, their arms behind their backs.

'What are they doing?' asked Fangy.

'They're trying to think,' said Meaty.

Then Abbiewail stopped and said brightly, 'I've got it.' The others looked at her.

'No, maybe not.' She continued to walk about.

Grimly stopped, then the others. 'Perhaps we could . . . no I don't think so.'

They went back to pacing the floor.

'Aunties?' Hatti called.

'Not now,' said Abbiewail. 'We're thinking.'

'I've got it,' said Scarea stopping abruptly. The other two sisters who were following behind bumped into her.

'Must you walk so close behind me, Abbiewail?' scolded Scarea.

'Don't blame me . . . you shouldn't have stopped like that.'

'Please, sisters, must we quarrel at a time like this . . .?'

'Well, she started it,' Abbiewail complained.

'Aunt Scarea?' Hatti called.

'What is it, child?' Scarea snapped.

'Well I think I understand it now. Flawless

and Rosalind are not in Salem, Massachusetts but are in Roswell, New Mexico.'

'So?' Abbiewail demanded.

'We could find out about Roswell on the Internet, then we could go there and try and rescue them.'

'That's a very good idea,' said Scarea.

'Well thought out,' said Grimly.

'I told you that kid had brains,' said Meaty.

'Will someone please tell me what the Internet is?' Abbiewail asked.

'Come to the studio and I'll show you,' said Hatti, 'if that's okay with Aunt Scarea.'

'Of course it is, my dear.'

'This I've got to see,' said Grimly.

'Me too,' said Abbiewail.

They all hurried to the studio. Hatti sat at the computer and having connected up to the Internet, she began to type.

'What are you clicking with your finger?' asked Grimly.

'Oh it's a mouse,' said Hatti.

'A mouse!' Grimly shrieked. 'Where is the wretched thing?' She hopped up on a chair. 'It's all right,' said Scarea. 'The mouse is part of the PC.'

'I knew that,' said Abbiewail.

Grimly got off the chair and smiled awkwardly. 'Now where were we?'

'Looking for Ross's Well?' said Abbiewail as she stared at the screen.

'It's Roswell,' said Scarea. 'It's important to get things right.'

Abbiewail pulled a face at her sister's remark.

'Here we are,' said Hatti brightly.

Scarea began to read off the screen. 'Roswell, New Mexico, 2nd July 1947. An unidentified flying object was found at MacBrazel's Ranch, south of Corona. The disc-shaped craft was struck by lightning and the debris from it was widely scattered about the ranch. Witnesses claim to have seen creatures who were not of this world.'

'Wow!' said Hatti.

'How amazing!' said Scarea.

'What's this got to do with Flawless and Rosalind?' asked Abbiewail.

'Don't you see?' said Boris. 'What you heard in the crystal ball was a call for help. Your relations have been abducted.'

'Oh how exciting,' Abbiewail cackled.

'It's just like the *X-Files*.' Her sisters stared hard at her. 'Oh what I mean is, it's terrible! Something must be done immediately if not sooner!'

'You're right, sister,' said Grimly, patting her on the back.

'Well, no time to waste,' said Scarea. 'I'm off to pack a bag.'

A few minutes later they were all ready.

'We better stick together,' said Grimly. 'Just in case we get abducted by aliens too.' She giggled nervously.

'You stay and mind the house,' Scarea said to Chompy and Fangy. 'Meaty and Boris can fly ahead and scout around.'

'Us two?' said Meaty looking at the raven.

'Yes,' she insisted. 'Is that clear?'

'Clear as mud,' chuckled Boris.

'Seems an awfully long way away,' Meaty grumbled. 'We better have ourselves a second breakfast,' he whispered to the raven.

They flew into the kitchen and finished the scraps on the table.

'Maybe I should have a little bird nap after all that food,' suggested Meaty. Scarea glared at him. 'On second thoughts I feel quite refreshed and look forward to this very, very long flight. Are you ready Boris?'

'Ready and willing!' the raven replied.

'Goodbye,' said Scarea. 'Do take care.'

They took flight from her bedroom window.

'Are we all ready?' asked Grimly anxiously as she grabbed her broom and magic wand.

'I'm ready,' said Abbiewail, holding a carpet bag and her broom. 'Plenty of goodies in here,' she patted the bag. 'In case we get hungry.'

'Let's not dilly-dally,' said Scarea. 'We really should go, there's no time to waste.'

'Listen to her,' snapped Abbiewail. 'I was ready before you.'

'You were not,' Scarea insisted.

'I was,' growled Abbiewail.

'Sisters, please, this arguing is setting a bad example for dear Hatti,' Grimly scolded.

'I don't mind,' said Hatti. 'It's fun to watch.'

'Well never mind them,' said Grimly. Then she looked at Hatti. 'Oh dear,' she said. 'What about you? You've got school today.'

'Don't worry about me, Auntie Grimly. I'll head off to Roswell after school.' Then she added, 'After all it is Friday.'

'Friday,' said Abbiewail thoughtfully. 'There's a great late night movie on tonight, *The Bride of Frankenstein*. I'll quickly hurry to record it on the video.'

Scarea gave a look of disapproval and got onto her broom. 'I'm off, follow after me.' And with that, she flew out the window.

'Come along, Abbiewail,' shouted Grimly.

'See you later, Hatti dear. Don't forget to bring your lunch to school.'

'It's packed,' said Hatti.

'Cheerio!' Grimly shot out the front door and over the trees.

'Wait for me,' yelled Abbiewail as she jumped onto her broom. 'See you later, Hatti.'

Hatti waved goodbye as she watched the three aunts fly high over the forest. Then she picked up her lunch and went off to school.

Hatti found it very difficult to concentrate in class. She couldn't help thinking about Flawless and Rosalind being kidnapped by aliens. Miss Baker, her teacher, accused Hatti of daydreaming in class and complained that she must be watching too much television and getting to bed far too late. Hatti couldn't tell Miss Baker what was really going on.

When school was over Hatti hurried to the local library and managed to find a book on the unexplained, all about strange and mysterious happenings. She found a whole section on Roswell called the Roswell File.

2nd July 1947: During a violent storm in Roswell, New Mexico, a rancher called MacBrazel hears an explosion that is too loud for thunder.

3rd July 1947: MacBrazel and friend find widely scattered debris and a big hole in the ground.

6th July 1947: Rancher MacBrazel takes sample of debris to police.

7th July 1947: Army takes samples to Fort Worth, Texas.

8th July 1947: Radio station in Roswell tells of a flying disc that crashed between Corona and Roswell.

9th July 1947: Military officials say crash was only a weather balloon.

1950: Secret memo to director of FBI, J. Edgar Hoover, says that three saucers each carrying three aliens were recorded in New Mexico.

'Wow!' cried Hatti. 'This is the real *X-Files*.'

People sitting at their desks looked over at Hatti; they seemed very cross. She quickly returned the book back to the shelf and left the library. She waved her magic wand over herself. 'Do your magic! Guide my broom to Roswell in New Mexico to my aunts.'

*   *   *

Meaty and Boris circled high in the sky. They could see tall mountains and the sharp peaks of the American west below.

'I'm hungry again,' said Meaty.

'Me too,' said Boris. 'Let's go and rest for a bit on one of those pointed rocks. How about that one over there, shaped like an eagle's head.'

'I'll race you down,' said Meaty. They circled and flapped to descend.

The raven landed first. 'I won,' he said proudly as Meaty joined him a few minutes later.

The vulture stretched his wings and preened his feathers a little. They settled down and looked around.

'Not much happening around here,' said Boris. 'Not even a restaurant or a shop to get something to eat.'

'Let's not talk about food,' sighed Meaty. 'It only makes me hungry.'

'Well you mentioned being hungry first,' the raven retorted.

'Oh yes, so I did. I wonder how far this Roswell place is?' Meaty mused.

'I don't know,' said Boris. 'But that turkey vulture we met earlier said it was in this direction.'

'Yes,' said Meaty. 'He said to fly over seven mountains, turn right at the gorge and across the desert, that we wouldn't miss it.'

'That's what he said all right,' Boris agreed.

'I can't remember if we've flown over six or seven mountains, can you?' asked Meaty.

'Well no,' said the raven. 'I thought you were counting – I was admiring the scenery.'

'Oh that's great, admiring the scenery when we've such an important mission ahead of us. Besides,' added Meaty, 'the sooner we get to that town the sooner we get food.'

'And I don't know about you but I fancy some Mexican food. Mmm, I can taste it already . . .' said Boris, closing his eyes, ' . . . the tacos and the tortilla chips . . .'

'Will you stop talking about food,' Meaty grumbled.

'Okay,' agreed Boris. Then he said brightly, 'Let's play a game while we're sitting here.'

'I'm too tired,' said Meaty. 'All that flying has me exhausted as well as hungry. Oops, I shouldn't mention being hungry.'

'You don't have to move,' said Boris. 'Only squawk or shout. And see how many echoes can be heard back. Look, I'll show you.' Boris took a deep breath. Then let out a loud croaking sound. They could hear the echo. Once! Twice! Three times!

'Hey, that's cool,' said Meaty. 'Let me try.' He took a deep breath and was just about to let out a squawk when Boris stopped him. 'What's up?' he demanded.

'Look! There! In the sky!' Boris pointed with his wing. 'What is it?'

'It's only one of those frisbies that kids throw around,' snapped Meaty.

'But no kid could throw a frisby that high,' Boris insisted.

'Yes you're right,' said Meaty. 'And it's coming closer.'

'It's the biggest frisby I've ever seen,' said a rather nervous Boris.

'You don't think it's one of those UFOs?' Meaty asked. He was trembling all over.

'It does look awfully like a flying saucer, the type you see in those science fiction movies.'

'Let's get out of here,' said Meaty.

They both took flight.

Suddenly a pink beam of light shot out from the underneath of the spacecraft and struck the vulture.

'Aahh, I'm shot,' said Meaty. 'Goodbye Boris! Goodbye world!' And with that he vanished in front of Boris's eyes.

Boris flew as fast as he could to get away
from the UFO but he too was hit with a beam
of pink light and disappeared.

*   *   *

'Hurry up sisters,' said Scarea. 'We want to get there by nightfall.'

'We've been going as fast as we can,' snapped Abbiewail. 'I just need to rest awhile.'

'My, it's hot,' said Grimly. 'Anyone fancy an ice cream?'

'I'd like a knickerbocker glory,' said Abbiewail.

'You think about nothing but your stomach,' said Scarea.

'Well, at least I don't spend all the time looking in the mirror admiring myself like someone not a million miles away.'

'Well at least I don't crack mirrors when I look in them,' Scarea retorted.

'What's that supposed to mean?' Abbiewail demanded.

'Sisters, please stop all the squabbling,' Grimly snapped. Then she began to laugh.

'What's so funny?' Abbiewail asked.

Grimly pointed to the end of her broom.

While they had stopped, a red-tailed hawk had landed on the broom and was perched at the base.

'Clear off!' yelled Abbiewail waving her arms.

The hawk squawked loudly and flew away.

'Oh dear, you frightened it,' Grimly scolded.

'Well, it shouldn't just drop out of the sky like that and land on my new broomstick.'

'It's an endangered species,' said Scarea.

You'll be an endangered species if you keep on having a go at me!' Abbiewail growled.

'Sister Abbiewail, I'm shocked,' said Grimly. 'If Mama was here she'd make you wash out your mouth with such talk.'

'I was just kidding,' said Abbiewail.

'Sisters, look! A town up ahead,' said Scarea.

'We must be there,' said Grimly excitedly. 'Now, let's all act normally when we arrive.'

'Here we are, flying in on broomsticks and you want us to act normally,' Abbiewail quipped.

They began to pick up speed, flying low just above the houses and stores until they could see a sign 'Welcome to Roswell'. A policeman on a motorbike caught sight of them. He got such a fright that he lost control of his bike and crashed into a pond.

'There! Look!' said Abbiewail pointing to an ice cream parlour.

They swooped down, parked their broomsticks and went into the parlour.

'Howdy y'awl!' said a large round jolly lady. 'Strangers in these parts?'

'How did you guess?' Grimly asked.

The lady winked and said, 'What can I get you guys?'

'We're not guys, we're women like you,' said Abbiewail.

'Don't mind her,' said Scarea. 'I'll have

some mint ice cream with some fresh fruit.'

'I'll have an ice cream float,' said Grimly, 'with chocolate, strawberry and vanilla ice cream and some cream.'

'I'll have a knickerbocker glory,' said Abbiewail. 'And make it a jumbo one.'

'Good choice,' said the waitress. 'Those desserts are out of this world.'

They sat down to eat their desserts but Abbiewail just stared at hers.

'What's the matter, sister dear?' said Scarea. 'Is it not big enough?'

'I'm not eating that,' she complained.

'Why ever not?' Grimly asked.

'I'm not eating alien ice cream,' snapped Abbiewail.

'What on earth are you talking about?' asked Grimly.

'You heard her, the desserts are out of this world.' Grimly and Scarea broke into hoots of laughter. 'What's so funny?' Abbiewail asked.

Just then a very wet policeman entered, waving his gun and a pair of handcuffs.

'Don't move,' he said, nervously pointing his gun. 'I know who you are, aliens.'

'Just because we're not from America there's no need to call us aliens,' said Grimly.

'Don't move,' he insisted. 'You can't fool me, dressed up in those ridiculous witch costumes.'

'How dare you be so insulting about our attire!' Scarea said. 'And it's rude to point, especially a gun.'

'You tell him,' said Abbiewail.

Scarea clicked her fingers and his gun turned into a banana. She clicked her fingers again and turned his uniform into a circus clown outfit. The lady behind the counter fainted and the policeman turned around and ran out of the store shrieking.

'Now we can have our desserts in peace,' Grimly said. 'Then we should head out to the desert.'

'That's funny,' Abbiewail chuckled. 'Dessert! Desert! Get it?'

'Just eat up,' sighed Scarea.

*   *   *

'What a beautiful starry night,' said Scarea.

'Lovely indeed,' Grimly agreed.

'Pity it's so cold,' Abbiewail complained.

'Who would have thought that the desert could be so cold at night. Still, it's fun to camp out,' Grimly chuckled.

'Let's get a camp fire started,' Scarea suggested.

'Good idea.' Abbiewail was about to wave her magic wand and make a nice big log fire.

'No dear,' said Grimly. 'Let's do it properly. Let's collect some firewood just like folk do in those western movies.'

'There's no wood around here,' said Abbiewail.

'There's sagebrush and tumbleweed,' said Scarea.

'Well if you two are so intent on making a fire the old-fashioned way, go right ahead. I'll get the supper ready,' suggested Abbewail.

Grimly smiled at her sisters saying, 'Let's try and look the part.' She waved her wand over Abbiewail then over Scarea and finally over herself. 'That's better,' she grinned.

Abbiewail was dressed like a cowgirl with a ten-gallon hat. Scarea looked very smart in her black and white gear. Grimly had a Mexican sombrero and a poncho. They all broke out into hoots of laughter at their appearance. Grimly and Scarea went away to collect firewood. There were lots of clumps of wood and twigs lying about. They both arrived back with two big bundles in their arms.

'We'll have enough for a nice big fire to burn all through the night,' said Grimly.

Abbiewail's jaw dropped open in horror as she watched her sisters return.

'What is it my dear? You look like you have seen a ghost!' Grimly wondered.

'Aaahhh . . . Snnn . . . Aahh!' stammered Abbiewail.

'Whatever is the matter?' snapped Grimly.

Then suddenly Scarea shrieked.

'Now what's up with you?' Grimly complained.

Grimly looked at the wood she had collected only to discover that she had picked up a nest of diamond-back rattlesnakes. They were wriggling about in her arms. She screamed and threw the snakes into the air.

43

The sisters hugged each other in fright as the snakes slithered away in annoyance.

'I think we'll light the fire Abbiewail's way.'

Abbiewail took aim at the ground, said a few magic words and a beautiful log fire appeared with a ring of rocks around it.

'That's much better,' all three agreed.

They settled down around the fire and enjoyed some supper. Later Abbiewail toasted sticky marshmallows over the flames.

'This is fun,' Grimly smiled broadly as she popped a marshmallow into her mouth.

'First time for me to camp outdoors like this,' Abbiewail admitted.

'It's the same for all of us dear,' said Scarea. A distant coyote could be heard howling in the dark.

'Isn't this just like one of those good ol' westerns,' said Grimly, 'where the hero rides into camp and is offered coffee and beans for supper.'

'Yes,' said Abbiewail excited as she pulled out her wand. 'Who would you like to see? The Duke?'

Grimly nodded enthusiastically, so her sister conjured up John Wayne.

He walked in from the darkness holding his horse by the reigns. 'Howdy ladies. Y'awl better keep a look out for Comanches.'

Grimly shrieked with laughter. 'Isn't he handsome?'

'I'd prefer James Stewart to rescue me,' said Abbiewail. She waved her wand again and suddenly James Stewart appeared alongside John Wayne.

'No, it should be Clint Eastwood,' insisted Scarea. She clicked her fingers and Clint Eastwood appeared.

'How about Roy Rogers,' said Abbiewail. 'And Gene Autry.'

'Burt Lancaster and Anthony Quinn. Kirk Douglas and Rex Allen,' added Grimly with glee.

Suddenly there were cowboy movie actors all around the campfire. Then a cross-looking man appeared with a patch over one eye.

'Do you mind, ladies? I'm trying to make a movie with these guys.'

'Oh very well,' said Scarea. She clicked her fingers and they all disappeared.

'Who was that old grumpy boots?'

'That was John Ford the famous film director. Oh I'd sure like to see that movie with all those fine actors in it . . .'

'Never mind all that. Let's have some music to pass the night away.' Scarea conjured up Jimmie Rodgers. He began to yodel the "Blue Yodel Number 9" as he sat on a rock with his guitar.

'What about Marty Robbins?' said Abbiewail. 'And Jim Reeves.'

'Let's have Patsy Cline and Tammy Wynette,' added Grimly. But before she could wave her wand, she was interrupted.

'Look over there!' said a worried Scarea. 'There's something moving very fast across the night sky.'

'Ahhh!' shrieked Abbiewail.

'Sorry, Mr. Rodgers, no time to listen to you but thanks for appearing.' Scarea clicked her fingers and the singer was gone.

'Let's hide,' said Grimly. They hurried into the tent and lay huddled together in the dark.

They heard a swoosh sound and then there was movement outside.

'There's somebody or something outside,' Abbiewail whispered.

'I hope it's had its supper,' said Grimly.

They could see the shadow of a small creature just outside the tent. Abbiewail was about to scream when Hatti appeared around the tent flap.

'Hi everyone,' she smiled. 'I hope I didn't wake you.'

'No,' snapped Abbiewail. 'You nearly made us jump out of our skin.'

'We're so pleased it's you, dear, and not some creature from outer space,' said Grimly.

'Yes, that's true, Hattie,' said Abbiewail. 'Sorry for snapping at you.'

'Oh, that's all right Auntie.'

'Let me make you some toasted marshmallows . . . they're delicious.'

'Great,' said Hatti.

They all sat outside again looking at the beautiful night sky.

Scarea gave a big yawn. 'Oh I'm so sleepy. I wonder if this is all some practical joke, this thing about Flawless and Rosalind being abducted by aliens.'

'Aliens are real,' said Abbiewail. She pointed to the sky. 'The truth is out there.'

'You watch too much TV,' Scarea retorted.

'I do not, it's mainly videos,' said Abbiewail. 'Except quiz shows and late night movies.'

'Look,' said Hatti pointing skywards.

'Where?' said Grimly. 'Oh yes, I see.'

A small circular-shaped object could be seen zigzagging across the night sky.

'Oh, wow!' said Abbiewail. 'That's it. That's what I saw in my crystal ball. Look at all those beautiful coloured lights.'

Suddenly it came to an abrupt halt. Then

three circular shapes shot from the vessel.

'Ahhh!' shrieked Grimly. 'They're firing giant balls at us.'

Hatti and Grimly hid behind a rock, while Abbiewail and Scarea took cover behind a cactus. The three balls shot like rockets towards the ground.

'Oh dear, what will we do?' said Grimly.

'I don't think we should do anything, Auntie, just watch and see what happens,' Hatti suggested.

When the shiny balls hit the ground, instead of smashing or exploding they began to bounce just like a child's rubber ball. Bounce, bounce, bounce. Over the tent, over the cactus, up and down, then side to side, all the while still bouncing.

'What the dickens is going on?' asked Scarea.

The bouncing balls started to slow up, but then began spinning like spinning tops.

Finally they stopped. Hatti and the others moved nervously towards them. As they got closer the lights inside the balls began to disappear only to reveal shapes.

'I can't look,' squealed Grimly. 'The balls are full of creatures with several eyes and lots of arms . . . and they look all gooey.'

'They're gooey all right, but not aliens. It's Meaty, Boris, Flawless and Rosalind.'

'What?' said Grimly opening her eyes.

She could see her cousins Flawless and Rosalind. They were in separate balls, and covered in a slimy substance. Meaty and Boris were together and looked just as messy.

'What happened to them? How did they get captured by goo?' wondered Abbewail.

Hatti went over to one of the balls and touched it. It felt like a rubber substance but it wasn't rubber.

'Could you please get me out of this?' Flawless pleaded.

'Don't worry, dear,' said Grimly. 'We'll have you out in a jiffy.'

'Stand aside,' said Scarea. She clicked her fingers at the balls. Nothing happened.

'Let me try,' said Abbiewail pulling out her wand. 'For important jobs you need a wand.'

She pointed her wand at the balls and said a few magic words, but still nothing happened.

'Let's all try together,' suggested Grimly.

They all aimed their wands. But nothing seemed to be able to penetrate the substance.

'How very odd,' said Scarea. 'It's most unusual for magic to let us down like this. It must be some kind of alien substance.'

'Did someone mention alien?' a small squeaky voice sniggered.

'Who said that?' Grimly asked.

'Aaagh!' shrieked Abbiewail. 'Over there!'

From the darkness a greenish light could be seen moving towards them. As it got closer they could see it was a creature from another world. An alien. Grimly screamed.

'Good evening, earthlings,' the creature said. 'I am the all powerful Vizwiz from the planet Upos.'

'I don't care where you're from,' snapped Abbiewail. 'Please free our relatives and pets immediately if not sooner.'

'Nobody tells me what to do. I am of a superior race than you, earthling.'

'So you think you're so smart? Well let me tell you, buster, anything you can do we can do better,' said Abbiewail.

The creature laughed loudly. 'Very well, I will challenge you to a duel.'

'Name your weapons,' said Abbiewail.

The alien tapped his head. 'Brain power. We will have a contest tomorrow at sunrise and we'll see who is the smartest.'

'You're on,' growled Abbiewail.

'Hold on,' said Scarea. 'What's the subject?'

'The movies,' said Abbiewail. 'I'm sure I'll beat him,' she whispered to Grimly.

'No,' said the alien. 'The universe. If you win I'll let your friends go free and I will not take over your planet.'

'What?' said Scarea. 'Take over the planet?'

The alien nodded. 'Until tomorrow,' he laughed nastily. Then he hurried away and into his spaceship. They watched him speed away over the desert and into the night sky.

'What will we do?' asked Grimly. 'We cannot let creatures like him take over the planet, they're not human!'

'Why did you agree to such a challenge?' Scarea snapped at Abbiewail.

'I didn't agree to anything,' Abbiewail said.

'Yes, you did,' Scarea insisted.

'Please, sisters, let us not argue at a time like this,' said Grimly. 'We need to put on our thinking caps and find a way to get our dear cousins out of those bubbles.'

'I think they're balls,' said Abbiewail. 'Bubbles don't bounce.'

'Oh whatever . . .' sighed Grimly. 'Let's think about this,' she said as she paced up and down.

Scarea began to walk behind her and then Abbiewail followed them. They rubbed their chins, scratched their heads, even pulled at their hair. It was no use; they just couldn't come up with any solutions.

'I have an idea,' said Hatti who was watching them pace up and down.

'What is it dear?' asked Grimly.

'Music,' said Hatti brightly.

'Now, dear,' said Scarea, 'I know you're trying to help but we don't feel like listening to music at this moment in time.'

'But, Aunt Scarea, I think the balls may have been made by bending sound waves.'

'I've never heard anything so ridiculous in all my life,' said Abbiewail.

'Look at Meaty nodding his head,' said Grimly.

'Meaty always nods when he's nervous,' said Scarea.

Meaty shook his head.

'Now he's shaking his head from side to side,' said Abbiewail.

'Well it wouldn't hurt to try,' said Grimly. 'To test Hatti's theory.'

'Oh very well,' said Abbiewail. 'I'll conjure up some music.' She waved her wand and a jukebox appeared in the sand.

'What's that?' asked Grimly looking at the flashing lights.

'It's a jukebox,' said Abbiewail. 'It plays music.'

'Music,' sighed Scarea. 'Why didn't you conjure up the Boston Symphony Orchestra or Yehudi Menuhin?'

'Because it's my choice,' snapped Abbiewail.

'Where can you plug it in?' asked Scarea.

'I thought of that too,' Abbiewail grinned as she plugged the jukebox into a power pack. 'Oh I'll need a nickel or a dime to play the jukebox.'

Scarea clicked her fingers and coins appeared in her hands. 'Here,' she said handing Abbiewail the coins. 'And hurry up.'

'Don't rush me,' said Abbiewail reading the songs in the jukebox. 'Carl Perkins, Ricky Nelson, Fats Domino, The Everly Brothers, Buddy Holly. Ah, Elvis Presley, 'Blue Moon of Kentucky'. That was his first hit from Sun records.'

'We don't have time for a rock'n'roll history lesson,' snapped Scarea.

Soon the music began. Abbiewail started dancing and shaking her leg.

'I give up,' sighed Scarea. 'This is so silly.'

'Look, look,' said a very excited Grimly.

The bubbles began to slowly disappear.

Soon Flawless and Rosalind were free and then Boris and Meaty.

'Oh that's better,' said Flawless, giving a sigh of relief.

'Well done,' said Scarea to Hatti. 'That was a brilliant idea of yours.'

'And well done, Abbiewail,' said Hatti, 'for setting them free with an excellent choice of music.'

Grimly waved her wand over her cousins and removed the green slimy substance. Then she did the same to Meaty and Boris.

'Oh I feel almost normal again, and how lovely to see you all,' said Flawless. She and Rosalind hugged their cousins. Meaty and Boris stretched and flapped their wings, relieved to be free again.

Scarea made them all a lovely supper and the two cousins explained how they'd been abducted by the alien late one night while flying to New Mexico.

After supper Grimly suggested that everyone go to bed as they had a very important day ahead of them – the day of the duel.

'I think you should be the one to represent Earth,' said Grimly to Hatti.

'Me?' said an anxious Hatti.

'Yes, dear, after all you're still in school and you're used to answering difficult questions. Don't worry it'll be just like a school exam. Now I don't want to alarm you but if you lose, that little horror of an alien said that he would take over our planet. Sleep well, dear,' she said brightly.

Hatti sat there feeling very worried at the idea of her having to be the one to protect the planet from an alien invasion by using her brain power. Eventually she got up and went to her tent.

*   *   *

Abbiewail blinked awake then gave a big yawn. Outside the tent Scarea and Flawless were busy getting breakfast ready. Then Hatti emerged from her tent looking very tired.

'You look like you didn't sleep too well,' said Scarea.

'That's right, Auntie. I didn't.'

'Well, a good breakfast will help you start the day right.'

'Aunt Scarea, would it not be better if you conjured up a genius like Albert Einstein or Isaac Newton instead of me?'

'Nonsense, my dear, we all have perfect confidence in you.'

'Oh that's nice,' replied a very nervous Hatti.

The moment the sun rose over the desert, the UFO appeared in the sky. It zigzagged all over the place before landing beside them.

'Show off,' said Abbiewail as she watched the alien leave the spacecraft.

'Good morning, earthlings. I've come to take over the planet,' he sniggered.

'Not yet, buster,' said Abbiewail staring him in the eye.

'Oh very well. Let's have the contest then, but you're wasting your time. My brain is superior to any earthling's.'

'We'll just see about that,' said Abbiewail.

'Who is to represent your planet?'

Scarea gently pushed Hatti forward.

'Her?' said the alien.

'Yes,' snapped Scarea. 'Our niece, Hatti.'

'Hatti? What a ridiculous name,' jeered the alien.

'Listen, mister,' said Meaty. 'You have a nerve calling her name ridiculous with a name like Vizwiz. If I had a fist I'd punch you in the nose, if you had one.'

'That's telling him,' said Abbiewail.

'Oh can't we get on with the contest? I'm in a hurry to own your planet.'

'Who's going to set the questions all about the universe?' asked Grimly.

'I'm glad you asked me that.' The alien clicked his fingers and a large robot appeared from the spaceship and slowly made its way down beside him.

Abbiewail squealed with fright.

'I am MODEL 2025, the finest computer robot in the universe.'

'He's modest,' said Grimly.

'What happens next?' asked Hatti.

'One at a time we press any button on his chest and a question will be asked. If we answer it correctly he will say 'correct', if not he will say 'error'. The one who answers the ten questions correctly wins.'

'That seems simple enough,' said Scarea. 'I'll press first for us.'

'Oh I love quizzes,' said Abbiewail.

'Question one,' said the robot. 'For Hatti.' Hatti swallowed nervously. 'Name the nine planets in your solar system starting with the closest to the sun.'

'Go on, dear,' said Grimly. 'You show him.'

Hatti smiled. 'Mercury, Venus, Earth, Mars, Jupiter, Saturn, Uranus, Neptune and Pluto.'

'Correct,' said the robot.

They all cheered loudly and patted Hatti on the back.

'Your turn,' Abbiewail growled at the alien.

The alien pressed a button.

'Where would you find the asteroid belt in this solar system?'

'That's a hard question,' said Meaty.

'Between Mars and Jupiter,' answered the alien.

'Correct,' said the robot.

'Clever boots,' snapped Abbiewail.

Hatti pressed a button.

'What is the diameter of the planet earth?'

Hatti scratched her chin. '12,700 km or, if you prefer, 8,000 miles.'

'Correct.' There were more shouts and hoots from everyone.

The alien pressed for his question.

'Name the space probe that sent pictures of Mercury back to Earth?'

'MARINER 10, in 1974.'

'Correct,' said the robot.

Hatti's turn. 'When was Neptune discovered by scientists?'

'1846,' said Hatti.

'Correct.'

The alien looked very cross. He tried next.

'What is the smallest planet in this solar system?'

'Pluto, of course.'

'Correct.'

'In what state of America did a meteorite strike 40,000 years ago?'

'Arizona,' said Hatti.

'Correct.'

'Which is the largest galaxy, the Milky Way or Andromeda?'

'Andromeda,' said the alien. 'It's twice the size of the Milky Way.'

'Correct.'

'What planet has a beautiful ring and has more moons than any other planet in your solar system?'

'Saturn,' Hatti yawned.

They both continued to answer all the difficult questions put to them by the robot. And both got ten out of ten correct.

'All we can do now is have a tie-breaker,' said the alien.

'All agreed? Hatti? Are you listening?'

Poor Hatti was lying on the ground.

'What's up?' asked Grimly. 'Has our dear niece fainted?'

'No,' said Scarea bending over her. 'She's fallen asleep. Wake up, Hatti,' she urged.

'It's no use,' said Abbiewail. 'She's sleeping soundly.'

'Well I can't wait around,' said the alien. 'I shall just declare myself the winner.'

'Hold it one minute,' said Abbiewail. 'I'm stepping in to represent the planet.'

'You?' said Scarea in disbelief.

'Yes, me,' growled Abbiewail. 'I'll show this pesky alien.'

'Oh very well,' said the alien. He pressed a button.

'Name three of the ten brightest stars?'

'Sirius, Vega, Capella.'

'Correct.'

'I can name the rest,' the alien offered.

'It's okay, show off,' snapped Abbiewail.

'It's your turn,' said Scarea.

'Good luck,' encouraged the others.

'I'll be fine don't worry,' said Abbiewail. She pressed the button. 'Oh this is very exciting,' she chuckled.

'Who was the first earthling astronaut to walk on Earth's moon?'

'I know, I know,' shrieked Abbiewail, 'Tom Hanks.'

'Error.'

'What?' said Abbiewail. 'It's right! There's something wrong with your computer.'

'Error,' the robot repeated.

'Tom Hanks is an actor . . . he was in that film, *Apollo 13*,' sighed Scarea.

'I get the question now,' the alien grinned from ear to ear. 'It was Neil Armstrong on July 21st 1969 along with Edwin Aldrin.'

'Correct.'

'I won, I won!' The alien jumped about.

'What will we do now?' said Grimly. 'We've just given away the planet to an alien.'

'I was sure it was Tom Hanks,' said a very puzzled Abbiewail.

Then Hatti woke up. 'What's happened? Did I fall asleep?'

'You certainly did,' announced Grimly in a worried voice, 'and at the wrong time. The alien won the challenge and is going to take over the world.'

'Sorry Auntie,' mumbled a sleepy Hatti.

'Oh I'm not blaming you,' said Grimly.

'Look,' croaked Boris the raven, pointing with his wing at the sky.

'Another flying saucer,' wailed Scarea. 'They're invading the planet already.'

'That was quick,' said Abbiewail.

An even larger spacecraft appeared and flew in over the desert. The alien looked rather worried as the UFO landed alongside his own one. A door opened and two larger aliens could be seen coming down the steps of the craft.

'Vizwiz!' shouted one of the aliens. She sounded very cross. 'Didn't I tell you before

never to take your father's spaceship without his permission.'

'I see you took my robot as well,' scolded the other alien. 'You know I need it for work.'

'I'm sorry, Mummy and Daddy. I won't do it again,' apologised Vizwiz. 'I was only having a bit of fun.'

'Well I hope you weren't bothering these nice earthlings.'

'Well, he was actually,' said Abbiewail. 'He kidnapped our dear cousins and our pets. And threatened to take over the planet.'

'Is that true?' snapped his mother. Vizwiz nodded. She turned to Abbiewail.

'Please accept my apologies for my son's naughty behaviour.' Then she added. 'You know what thirteen-year-olds are like, they can be very trying at times.'

'Well it's really Flawless and Rosalind who deserve the apology.'

'Oh we forgive him,' they said together. 'As long as he doesn't do it again.'

Then they began to giggle. 'To tell you the truth,' said Flawless, 'the trip in the UFO was so exciting . . . and those bouncing balls . . .'

'It was out of this world,' agreed Rosalind.

This comment brought hoots of laughter.

'Well I'm glad that's settled with no hard

feelings,' said the alien father. 'Why don't you all come to Upos for a vacation? It's only twenty-six light years away.'

The witches looked at each other. They all nodded in agreement.

'Is there food there?' asked Meaty.

'Lots,' said Vizwiz.

'Let's go then,' he chuckled.

'We better get out of here soon, Mother,' smiled the alien, 'before the MIB arrive.'

'The Men in Black,' said Hatti to her aunts.

'Remember the night I brought you here on our first date?' said the alien to his wife.

'Will I ever forget it! It was a really stormy night and we caused such a fuss on Earth when we were spotted.'

'And the military let on it was a weather balloon, instead of giving the real explanation.'

This brought more laughter.

Hatti watched her aunties climb into the mothership. Then she went with Vizwiz and the robot into the smaller ship. As they shot off into the night sky and were whizzing past Mars, Vizwiz said he thought Hatti must be a genius answering all those difficult questions.

'Well to be honest I conjured up a book on astronomy and spent all night studying it. That's why I fell asleep earlier. I was so tired. So it's really you who's the clever one.'

'I have to confess I programmed the computer to ask those questions as I knew all the answers from my light years study class.'

They both broke out laughing

'Well at least we're all friends now,' said Hatti. Then she scratched her head. 'I have an idea.' She pulled out her wand and said a few magic words.

'What are you doing?' asked the alien.

'You'll see,' she retorted.

Next minute the jukebox appeared in the ship with its lights flashing. Vizwiz looked alarmed.

'It's okay, it's only a jukebox. It plays music. The music in it is a bit old-fashioned but it's good. I thought it might make a nice gift to your parents as a peace offering. You can tell them that this music was very popular around the time they first came to visit Roswell on planet earth.'

'That's a great idea. Thanks, Hatti.'

*   *   *

'This is truly amazing,' said Grimly, looking at all the lights and fancy controls in the mothership.

The others were staring at the millions of stars shooting by the window.

Then Scarea said, 'Of course you realise that when we arrive at Upos we will be considered aliens.'

'That's very true,' agreed Abbiewail. 'And who knows we may end up in an episode of the *X-Files*.'

'You mean the W-Files,' quipped Grimly. 'After all, we are witches.'

They all laughed loudly.

THE END